# Dear Parent:

Congratulations! Your child is taking the first steps on an exciting journey. The destination? Independent reading!

**STEP INTO READING®** will help your child get there. The program offers five steps to reading success. Each step includes fun stories and colorful art. There are also Step into Reading Sticker Books, Step into Reading Math Readers, Step into Reading Write-In Readers, Step into Reading Phonics Readers, and Step into Reading Phonics First Steps! Boxed Sets—a complete literacy program with something for every child.

## Learning to Read, Step by Step!

### Ready to Read  Preschool–Kindergarten
• big type and easy words • rhyme and rhythm • picture clues
For children who know the alphabet and are eager to begin reading.

### Reading with Help  Preschool–Grade 1
• basic vocabulary • short sentences • simple stories
For children who recognize familiar words and sound out new words with help.

### Reading on Your Own  Grades 1–3
• engaging characters • easy-to-follow plots • popular topics
For children who are ready to read on their own.

### Reading Paragraphs  Grades 2–3
• challenging vocabulary • short paragraphs • exciting stories
For newly independent readers who read simple sentences with confidence.

### Ready for Chapters  Grades 2–4
• chapters • longer paragraphs • full-color art
For children who want to take the plunge into chapter books but still like colorful pictures.

**STEP INTO READING®** is designed to give every child a successful reading experience. The grade levels are only guides. Children can progress through the steps at their own speed, developing confidence in their reading, no matter what their grade. Remember, a lifetime love of reading starts with a single step!

Thomas the Tank Engine & Friends™

CREATED BY BRITT ALLCROFT

Based on The Railway Series by The Reverend W Awdry.
© 2007 Gullane (Thomas) LLC.

Thomas the Tank Engine & Friends and Thomas & Friends are trademarks of Gullane
(Thomas) Limited. Thomas the Tank Engine & Friends and Design are Reg. U.S. Pat. & Tm Off.

HIT entertainment

All rights reserved. Published in the United States by Random House Children's Books,
a division of Random House, Inc., New York, and in Canada by Random House of Canada
Limited, Toronto.

STEP INTO READING, RANDOM HOUSE, and the Random House colophon are registered trademarks
of Random House, Inc.

www.stepintoreading.com
www.thomasandfriends.com

Educators and librarians, for a variety of teaching tools, visit us at
www.randomhouse.com/teachers

*Library of Congress Cataloging-in-Publication Data*
Gordon's new view / illustrated by Richard Courtney.
    p.   cm. — (Step into reading. A Step 1 book)
"Based on The railway series by the Rev. W. Awdry."
SUMMARY: Gordon, a very large blue engine, is annoyed when his view at the new train station
is obstructed.
ISBN 978-0-375-83978-8 (trade pbk.) — ISBN 978-0-375-93978-5 (lib. bdg.)
[1. Railroad trains—Fiction.] I. Courtney, Richard. II. Awdry, W. Railway series.
PZ7.G65948 2007  [E]—dc22  2006033859

Printed in the United States of America
10  9  8  7  6  5  4  3  2
First Edition

# Gordon's New View

Based on *The Railway Series*
by the Rev. W. Awdry

Illustrated by Richard Courtney

Random House 🏠 New York

Gordon was big.

Gordon was tall.

Gordon liked his view
from the Yard.

Gordon liked his view
from the stations, too.

He could see people.

People could see him.

"Gordon, you must go
to the new station,"
said Sir Topham Hatt.

Gordon rushed

to the new station.

He stopped inside.

There was no view.

Gordon could not see

the people.

They could not see him.

The next day,
Gordon was busy.
He pulled
the Express.

He rushed

to the Docks.

He raced back
to the new station.

He was in a hurry.

But his brakes were stuck.

# He could not slow down.

# Crash!

Gordon crashed

into the bumper.

# Smash!

Gordon smashed
into the wall.

Now people could see him.
But Gordon could not
see them.
His eyes were shut tight.

23

# The breakdown train pulled Gordon back.

"Gordon, go to the Works,"
said Sir Topham Hatt.

When Gordon came back,
he was fixed.

The wall was fixed, too.
It had
a new window.

# Gordon likes

# his new view.

# He can see people . . .

. . . and people can see him.

"Peep, peep!"